ANTHONY BROWNE

WILLY the WIZARD

CANDLEWICK PRESS

CAMBRIDGE, MASSACHUSETTS

First Candlewick Press edition 2003

Library of Congress Cataloging-in-Publication Data

Browne, Anthony, date.
Willy the wizard / Anthony Browne.
p.   cm.
Summary: Willy the chimpanzee loves to play soccer, but he is never picked
for a team until a stranger gives him some shoes that he is certain are magic.
ISBN 0-7636-1978-7
[1. Soccer—Fiction. 2. Chimpanzees—Fiction.] I. Title.
PZ7.B81984 Wl 2003
[E]—dc21   2002067698

2 4 6 8 10 9 7 5 3 1

Printed in Singapore

This book was typeset in Plantin.
The illustrations were done in watercolor, ink, and colored pencil.

Candlewick Press
2067 Massachusetts Avenue
Cambridge, Massachusetts 02140

visit us at www.candlewick.com

For Nicholas, Francesca, and Jacqueline

Willy loved soccer. But there was a problem—
he didn't have any cleats. He couldn't afford them.

Willy went eagerly to the practices every week. He ran and chased and hustled, but no one passed the ball to him. He was never picked for the team.

One evening, when Willy was walking home past the
old pie factory, he saw someone kicking a ball around.
The stranger was wearing an old-fashioned soccer uniform,
like the clothes Willy remembered his dad wearing.
But he was good. Very good.

Willy watched for a while, and when the ball came
over to him, he kicked it back. They played
silently together, passing the ball back and forth.

Then the stranger did something very odd.
He unlaced his cleats, took them off, and without
saying a word, he handed them to Willy.

Willy stared at them with wonder.

When he looked up,
no one was there.

Taking great care not to step
on any cracks in the sidewalk,
Willy took the cleats home.

He cleaned and polished
them until they looked new.

Then he went slowly upstairs, counting *every* step (sixteen), washed his hands and face *very* thoroughly, brushed his teeth for *exactly* four minutes, put on his pajamas (always the top first, always with *four* buttons fastened), used the bathroom, and dived into bed. (He had to be in bed before the flushing stopped, for who knows what would happen if he wasn't?) Every morning he repeated all of these actions in reverse. *Every* morning.

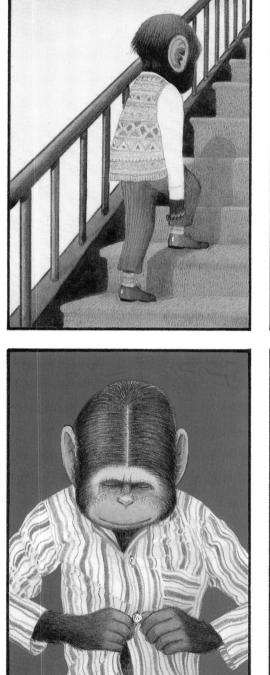

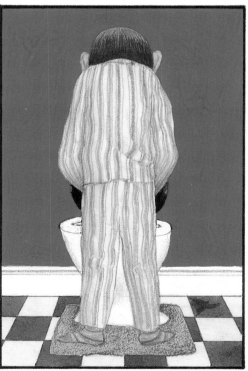

For the next soccer practice, Willy proudly
took along his cleats. But the other players
weren't exactly impressed . . .

. . . until they saw him play.

Wearing the old cleats, Willy was fantastic!

When the captain posted the
team for next Saturday's game,
Willy could hardly believe his eyes.

He was so pleased that he ran all the way home
(being very careful not to step on the cracks).

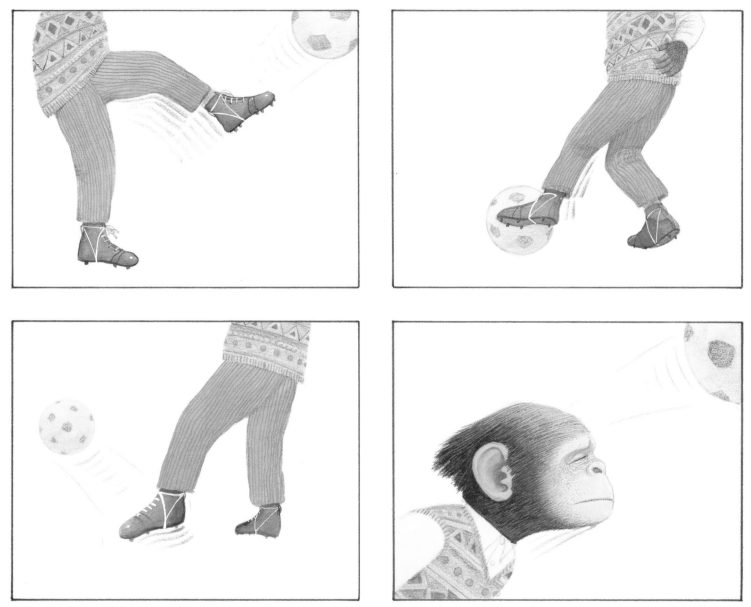

Every day Willy wore his cleats and practiced
shooting, dribbling, passing, and heading.
He got better and better. Willy was sure
his cleats were magic.

Every evening Willy wore his cleats and went
back to the old pie factory. There was something
curiously familiar about the stranger that made
Willy want to see him again. But he was never there.

On Friday night Willy went through his usual bedtime routine. He went slowly upstairs counting *every* step (still sixteen), washed his hands and face *very* thoroughly, brushed his teeth for *exactly* four minutes, put on his pajamas (the top first, with *four* buttons fastened), used the bathroom, and dived into bed before the flushing stopped. (Phew!)

But Willy was too excited to sleep.
Even when he drifted off, he had an
uncomfortable night, dreaming of disasters.

In the morning, he woke up with a start.

It was 9:45 and the game started at 10!

He leaped out of bed,

threw on his clothes,

raced down the stairs,

and dashed out the door.

Willy ran all the way to the soccer field.

When he got there, the other players had already
changed. The captain threw Willy his uniform, and
he put it on. Then the awful thought struck him . . .
HE HAD FORGOTTEN HIS CLEATS!
Someone found him another pair.
"Y-you don't understand . . ." he said, but the
team had already gone onto the field.

The crowd's roar turned to laughter when Willy emerged from the dressing room. Willy grinned, but inside he felt angry.

The game started. Willy was amazed how fast it was. Within minutes the opposition had scored. One to nothing! From the kickoff, the ball shot out to Willy on the wing. He didn't have time to think—he just ran with the ball at his feet.

Willy was magic. The ball seemed to be attached to him by an invisible thread. He dribbled past three opponents and sent in a perfect cross. GOAL!

It seemed that Willy could do no wrong.
Every time he got the ball, the opposition was
mesmerized. The teams were very evenly
matched. With seconds to go, the score was still
1–1. The ball was passed to Willy on defense. He
beat one player, then another, and another, and
another, until he got past the whole team.

Only the goalkeeper to beat. The goalie
was huge and the net looked tiny.
Could Willy do it?

He could! The crowd was spellbound as Willy
conjured up the perfect shot. GOALLLLL!!!

"WILLY THE WIZARD! WILLY THE WIZARD!"
chanted the crowd.

Later, on the way home,
Willy thought about the
cleats and the stranger.
And he smiled.

DATE			
5-26